Freddie
meets Freddie

Foreword by Andrew Flintoff M.B.E

I am delighted to be writing the foreword for this book; not only because of little Freddie the ball, but I know that Chris Cowdrey and I share the same beliefs – we play cricket for the love of the game. There is plenty of fun in this book!

It provides us with a memory of one of the greatest Ashes Series of all time in 2005, but more importantly proceeds of this book will go towards a charitable cause close to my heart.

The *Chance to shine* is a wonderful cause set up to secure a brighter cricketing future within state schools. Too many young people have been deprived of the chance to play cricket and to broaden their learning as young people. Cricket gives them a *Chance to shine.*

To all children who read this book, I hope you will enjoy your cricket. It is a great game, especially if you are in a team which plays for each other at all times. You need a bit of luck in sport to be in the right place at the right time. My meeting with little Freddie in the book proves this point - I am sure you will enjoy the adventures of a very lucky ball!

****

Chance to shine
BRINGING CRICKET TO STATE SCHOOLS

Chris Cowdrey is an Ambassador for *Chance to shine*, the Cricket Foundation's campaign to regenerate cricket in State Schools. A donation will be made to the Charity from sales of this book and copies will be presented to many of the children benefiting from *Chance to shine*.

Supported by

Freddie
meets Freddie

by Chris Cowdrey
for Julius & Fabian

Illustrated by Tony Brooks

BLUE COW BOOKS

Billy had permission from his parents to have a new cricket ball - his first leather ball with a proper seam. The cricket master handed out the shiny red balls to the boys. Their school number was stamped on the ball with a branding iron so that they wouldn't get mixed up. Billy's was number 75.

Billy wanted him to have a name rather than just a number like the other balls, so he christened him 'FREDDIE.'

Billy loved Freddie. Every night he would polish him before he went to bed and Freddie always slept next to him on the pillow.

One day Freddie awoke with great excitement. Today was match day and he was to be the match ball. "Will I be a fast ball or a slow ball today, I wonder?" thought Freddie. He really wanted to be a spinner because Billy was a spin bowler.

The match began and after a while Freddie was exhausted. It was a hot day and all the bowlers were very fast. At last it was Billy's turn to bowl.

"Hi Freddie," said Billy, "they haven't looked after you very well have they?"

Before bowling his first ball, Billy gave him a good shine on his trousers. "Now Freddie, let's bowl a nice leg-spinner shall we?"

Billy spun him into the air; the batsman had a wild swing of the bat and as Freddie pitched he pushed off his right hand, spinning 12 inches past the bat. Freddie thought it was very funny. The batsman was furious.

However, next ball, he came running down the pitch before
Freddie had time to land and hoisted him high over the trees.

"Oh no," screamed Billy "I will never see Freddie again."

The little ball, number 75, flew out of the ground and bounced
down the street. A dog barked at him, a cat fled in fear.
Mr Lewis, the man in the china shop yelled, "Stop, stop,
dead-ball, stop" but it was too late …

… CRASH, CLATTER, CRASH … Mr Lewis was very cross and kicked Freddie out of the shop. The local policeman came to inspect the damage. "We seem to have had a BALL in a china shop!" he said

Meanwhile, Freddie had bounced off the bonnet of a car, knocked the vicar off his bicycle and spun unnoticed onto a double decker bus. As he lay under a seat, he heard someone ask where the bus was heading.

"London," said the conductor.
"Wow!" thought Freddie; he had never been to London.
"Next stop, Buckingham Palace."

Freddie swung his way down the bus striving for extra bounce,
in the hope that he might see the Queen out of the window.
But he was caught low down by the conductor.

"Well, well, little ball," he said, "now how did you get here,
I wonder?"

"I could hardly say a full toss on leg stump could I?"
chuckled Freddie.

At the bus stop the conductor tossed him into a litter bin for not having a ticket. Luckily it was full to the brim and he could see over the top. Freddie could see Buckingham Palace in all its splendour. The royal flag was flying and even a little ball knew what that meant – the Queen was at home.

When it went dark Freddie fell asleep only to be woken at 5 o'clock in the morning by the dustmen, who tipped him into the back of a huge lorry. What a bumpy ride it was through Hyde Park. He was just about at the end of his tether and in really bad shape, when he spotted these huge gates.

"Wow, the Grace Gates!" he thought "we're at Lord's Cricket Ground."

With great control Freddie spun off an old tin can and swung out of the lorry. After a few bounces he found the perfect line and length. He came to rest beside the entrance to the most famous cricket ground in the world.

Freddie sat quietly, minding his own business, when a big coach arrived carrying the Australian cricket team. A newspaper salesman cried out:

"Ashes preview ... read all about it ... Test Match starts tomorrow ... read all about it!"

"Wow, England versus the world champions at Lord's....if only I could get a ticket," thought Freddie.

After a while he was spotted by the groundsman returning from lunch. "Now little ball what are you doing here? You should be inside the ground, not outside."
"Quite right!" thought Freddie proudly.
"Mind you, I shouldn't think the Aussies will want a smelly thing like you. Come on, I will take you in anyway."

"Hooray!" thought Freddie

The groundsman hurled him across the nursery ground into a pile of other balls where the Australians were practising. Freddie wanted to play with them, but they didn't like him. Some held their noses because he smelled of the rubbish bin, others held their noses in the air because they were rather snooty.

"He is not a Test Match ball, he shouldn't be here," said one posh, shiny ball to another.

At that moment the fielding practice started and Freddie was put in the pile with all the others. The Aussie coach lofted him into the air and fast bowler Michael Kasprowicz caught him nicely before exclaiming loudly,

"Geez coach you've hit me a real skunk of a ball – he smells like a rubbish dump."

In a flash Kasprowicz threw him away into the distance with disdain. Poor Freddie lay on the grass sobbing, with tears rolling down his cheeks. My, how he missed Billy. He just wanted to go home – he loved Billy.

Then suddenly he realised how lucky he had been. He had ended up rolling out onto the middle of the main ground.

"Gosh, I might be able to see the Test Match after all," thought Freddie. In case anyone spotted him, he hid behind the pitch covers.

Just before nightfall, he was disturbed by the purring of an engine and he remembered that the cover at Lord's was no ordinary cover, it was a HOVER COVER. The time had come for the groundsman to move it to the middle to cover the Test Match pitch and it suddenly started to move. In order not to be spotted, Freddie had no option but to hop aboard.

"Wow, this is like flying first class on British Airways," Freddie thought as he flew out to the middle. In just three minutes the hover had arrived at its destination and the whole cricket square was covered for the night.

Freddie settled down for bed in his new 5 star accommodation, tucked up under the covers in the middle of Lord's Cricket Ground.

During the night there was a thunderstorm. Freddie was delighted for he was able to have a good wash. Then he settled down for some sleep, it had been a long day. He dreamt of his friend Billy.

He was awoken by a
buzz around Lord's.
It was full of people
and the sun was
blazing down.
Freddie was startled
by the sound of the
bell, which told him
there was five minutes
until the start of the
match. The umpires
were coming out on
to the ground.

"Perfect timing!"
thought Freddie and he
settled down for the
action on the boundary's edge.

Freddie had the best seat in the house and he wallowed in the
special atmosphere for five days.

"I wish Billy was here," he thought sadly.

Freddie was also sad that Australia won the match, but he had watched every single ball through his binoculars. At one stage he had spotted Michael Kasprowicz on the dressing room balcony. He thought to himself "One day Kaspa, I will get my own back on you for calling me a skunk!"

Then as Freddie settled down for some kip, he was picked up on the run and thrown into a bag. He had been caught one handed. For days he lay in the dark bag, where he cried and cried.

All he wanted was to go home to Billy.

Then at last the bag opened and Freddie rolled out onto the green grass.

"Wow, this isn't any old grass, this is Edgbaston and there are the Aussies … wow, I am at the 2nd Test Match" he shrieked.

Freddie settled down to watch Australia practice. They were kicking a football around to get warmed up for the match, when the great fast bowler Glenn McGrath trod on Freddie and twisted his ankle.

"OUCH" yelled Freddie, before rolling away to hide. He didn't want to be spotted or he would have been blamed for putting the bowler out of the match.

Glenn McGrath was taken away on a stretcher and Freddie found a perfect spot to hide in some grass cuttings. Freddie sat in awe watching the GREATEST TEST MATCH OF ALL TIME unfold in front of his very eyes.

Then, with England closing in on victory, an extraordinary thing happened. Australian superhero, Shane Warne hit the ball out to the boundary and it came to rest right beside Freddie.

"Hi, Test Match ball, how are you?" said Freddie, in awe of the big ball.
"Oh, oh, I'm exhausted. The pressure, the heat out there – I've got a terrible headache, I wish you could go out there instead of me."
"But I can, I can … I will," said Freddie.
"No way, you're only a little guy and besides, you're too shiny."
"Not really, I am normally dirty and smelly like a SKUNK – I could rub myself in the dirt and stick my chest out to look like an adult ball," pleaded Freddie.

"OK, buddy, let's try it. I will hide there in the grass - cover up your number in the dirt. If you get away with it, remember the Aussies don't like reverse swing, so lean onto your shiny side and duck your head before landing. Good luck little ball!"

"Call me Freddie – see you later"

The fielder picked up Freddie who was now in disguise and threw him into the bowler. Not just any old bowler, he thought, it was his hero, the great Freddie Flintoff.

"Wow" thought Freddie, as he gazed at Freddie.

"Now I know why the crowd were chanting Freddie …
Freddie … Freddie - it's for him not me!" laughed little Freddie.

As he was tossed from hand to hand on the way back to his
mark, Freddie was in seventh heaven. "If only Billy could see
me now," he thought, "I am a Test Match ball now."

But he was overawed by the occasion forgetting all he had
learned about bowling. He was hurt when a skier was dropped
by a player who the crowd called butterfingers, and he landed
on his head.

A short wide delivery resulted in a square cut to the boundary
and a plaster was needed to patch up the cut. A yorker dug out
and Freddie was left coughing and spluttering from all the dust.

"This Test Match cricket is tough. We can't get these AUSSIES
out; I had better start concentrating," thought Freddie as he
wiped the sweat off his brow with a rag.

From then on he remembered the advice he had been given from the real Test Match ball and he started to help Jones and Flintoff to reverse swing the ball. Little Freddie got his head down and dreamed that he was on the Cresta Run in St.Moritz, leaning one way, then the other. At the last minute he dropped his head to one side and he ducked in sharply. The Aussies were dumbfounded but he couldn't quite get them out.

"Me and Freddie keep appealing for LBW, but the umpire can't hear us," thinks the little ball.

So with the Aussies requiring 61 runs and England needing just 2 more wickets to win, the moment came for something unusual.

Flintoff released Freddie; the reverse swing took him towards leg stump, where Shane Warne tried to tickle him down the leg side. Although little Freddie was laughing hysterically, he still managed to pull Warne's leg. So much so that he nudged the stump with his foot, the bails fell off and he was out.

Hooray! Little Freddie's first Test wicket: "Warne - hit wicket, bowled Flintoff."

The last man walked in for Australia. It was the man with the funny name - Michael Kasprowicz. "My chance for revenge," thought Freddie "Skunk of a ball am I, Kaspa?" he yelled at the incoming batsman.

"Hey, hey, hey fellah," said Freddie Flintoff to his little friend, "we don't need to resort to sledging - we only need one more wicket to beat Australia, let's win it fair and square."

"OK FREDDIE," said Freddie

But Michael Kasprowicz and the mighty Brett Lee stood firm as the victory target was whittled down to under 10 runs. Freddie tried everything. Reverse swing, spinners, bouncers, over the wicket, round the wicket. Flintoff tried the slower ball where Freddie dropped anchor and put the brakes on but just missed the off stump on his way past.

Brett Lee hit him high into the air for what seemed a certain six but Freddie threw out the parachute and was able to fly back into play. He was maturing as a Test Match ball all the time.

Then with the match almost lost to Australia – just 2 runs to win – little Freddie's moment arrived. The big man Steve Harmison had Freddie in the palm of his hand and he turned to him and said, " Little buddy, you are about to go on a bit of a journey; you may be tired and it may hurt, but it might just make you a hero. I am going to smack you into the ground half way down the pitch, you will leap up into the air towards Kaspa's head and then it is up to you – OK?"

"OK, Harmy."

The trap was set and as Freddie pole-vaulted into the air he managed to give Kaspa a high five as he touched his glove on his way past. But, could he reach the keeper on the full?

"C'MON, JONESEY, C' MON DIVE, DIVE JONESEY!"
he yelled.

Freddie pulled in all his straps put his seat belt on and prepared for a soft landing into the gloves of Geraint Jones. Hooray, Kaspa was out and England had won. Freddie had done it! The crowd cheered and cheered and cheered.

Freddie knew Billy would be cheering at home and a tear ran down his face as suddenly he missed Billy more than ever. Brett Lee was also crying.

Flintoff went over to Lee to console him with a big bear hug, whilst Kasprowicz shook hands with little Freddie.

"What good sportsmanship," he thought, as someone had to lose in what had been the greatest Test Match of all time.

Freddie was put in the umpire's pocket against his will. When they got off the field, the umpire noticed there was something unusual about the match ball.

"Gosh, this ball has a number on it, number 75. We will be in trouble if anyone finds out that the ball was switched."

"Don't worry," said the other umpire, "I will take him home with me. My young boy, Tommy, loves cricket."

Freddie was disappointed for he wanted to stay with the England team or even better go back to Billy. Anyway, Tommy was a kind boy, who played with him all day long in the garden, before putting him away in the games room.

Fortunately for Freddie, there were lots of other balls around, who were all very friendly. They were amazed to hear of his adventure. He told them how desperately he wanted to go home and they immediately hatched a plan.

On Saturday, Tommy's school were playing an away match.
All the cricket balls would travel as practice balls. The match
was at Billy's school. They explained the plan to Freddie ...

"Ball number 20 has been selected as the match ball because he
is the shiniest and cleanest. If he gets injured, they will have to
use another ball. So, number 20 is going to pick his seam so

that he looks in bad shape and has to retire hurt. Then they will pick the next best looking ball. If you smarten yourself up Freddie, it could be you. That's the plan, good luck! "

Well, Freddie, the number 75, was beside himself when he arrived; he recognised his old home instantly. He bumped into 74 and 76 who were thrilled to see him and they told Freddie that Billy had been miserable ever since he left.

"What if Billy doesn't remember me and I am taken away in the bag again? How will he recognise me?" worried Freddie.

Number 20 did his job and just came apart at the seam. So the cricket master went over to the balls to select another one. He walked alongside them as they stood on parade. They had all rolled in the dirt deliberately, putting on miserable faces. Some pretended to ill. Then he came across Freddie, number 75, who shone like a beacon and was dressed in his favourite bow tie.

They all held their breath. Would he take the new ball? Surely Freddie would be picked. And YES he was – so far so good!

Billy was batting and it was up to Freddie to show him what he could do. He was the finest spinner of them all – everyone knew that. So, as the first delivery landed Freddie pushed off his right hand and beat the outside edge of Billy's bat; the perfect leg-spinner. The same thing happened again and again. On the fourth delivery he pushed off his left hand, spinning the other way, hitting Billy's leg stump. The perfect googly. Billy was out.

All the balls lay motionless as Billy stood angrily glaring at the spinning ball.

Suddenly his eyes lit up and Billy screamed with joy, "Hang on
a minute, I've only ever known one ball that could spin like that
– it can't be, can it? It can't be my little friend? …

… IT IS … Freddie you've come home, HOORAY …
HOORAY … HOORAY!

Billy and Freddie watched the rest of the Ashes series together
and when England regained the Ashes at the Oval only
Freddie knew how important his role had been. They watched
as the England players celebrated on an open top bus in
Trafalgar Square.

The Australians flew home and Freddie thought, "They were a great team those Aussies – even Kaspa, who turned out to be a really good guy."

He rested his head on the pillow.

"Night night Billy" .... "Night night Freddie."